HOW THINGS BEGAN

Mary Jean McNeil

Illustrated by Colin King
Designed by John Jamieson

Educational Adviser: Frank Blackwell

First published in 1975
Second printing 1977
Third printing 1979
Usborne Publishing Ltd
20 Garrick Street
London WC2E 9BJ, England
© Usborne Publishing Ltd 1975

Published in Canada by
Hayes Publishing Ltd
Burlington, Ontario

Published in the U.S.A.
by Hayes Books
4235 South Memorial Drive,
Tulsa, Oklahoma, U.S.A.

Published in Australia by
Rigby Limited
Adelaide, Sydney, Melbourne
Brisbane, Perth

Printed in Belgium
by Henri Proost
Turnhout, Belgium

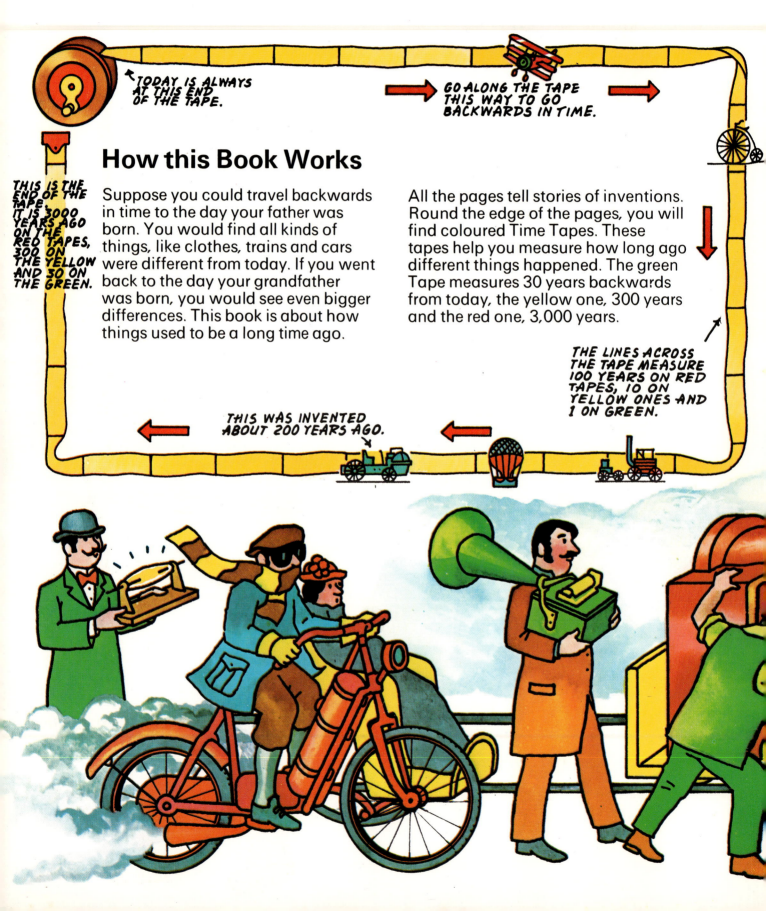

TODAY IS ALWAYS AT THIS END OF THE TAPE.

GO ALONG THE TAPE THIS WAY TO GO BACKWARDS IN TIME.

THIS IS THE END OF THE TAPE. IT IS 3000 YEARS AGO ON THE RED TAPES, 300 ON THE YELLOW AND 30 ON THE GREEN.

How this Book Works

Suppose you could travel backwards in time to the day your father was born. You would find all kinds of things, like clothes, trains and cars were different from today. If you went back to the day your grandfather was born, you would see even bigger differences. This book is about how things used to be a long time ago.

All the pages tell stories of inventions. Round the edge of the pages, you will find coloured Time Tapes. These tapes help you measure how long ago different things happened. The green Tape measures 30 years backwards from today, the yellow one, 300 years and the red one, 3,000 years.

THE LINES ACROSS THE TAPE MEASURE 100 YEARS ON RED TAPES, 10 ON YELLOW ONES AND 1 ON GREEN.

THIS WAS INVENTED ABOUT 200 YEARS AGO.

How Things Began

Contents

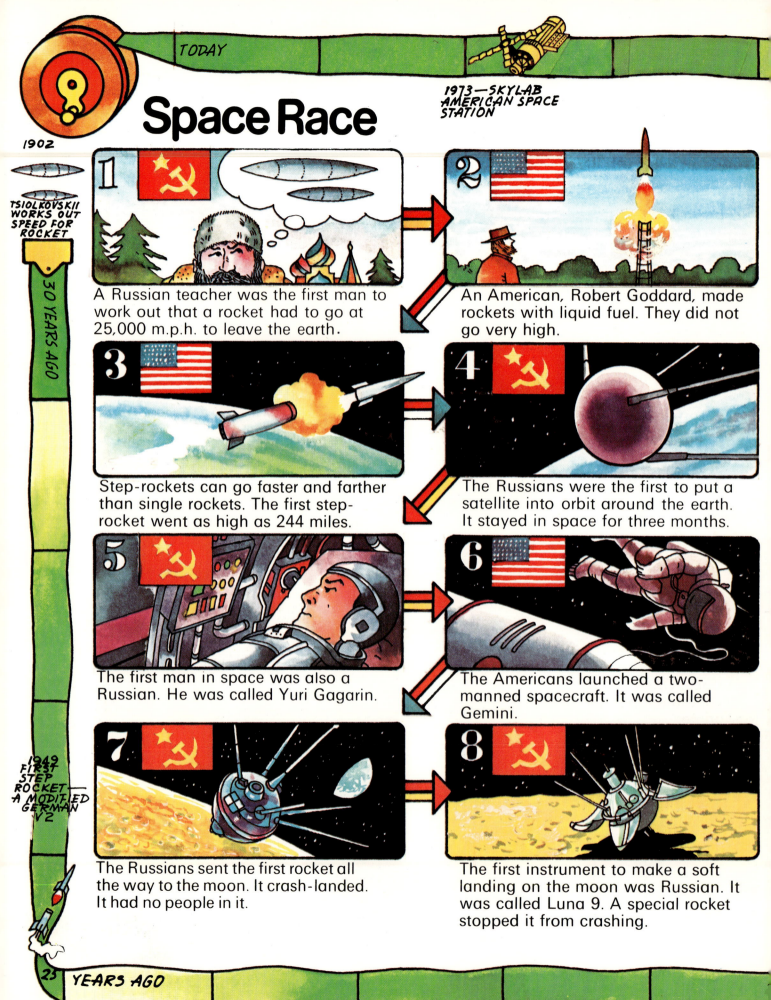

Space Race

1973—SKYLAB AMERICAN SPACE STATION

1902

TSIOLKOVSKII WORKS OUT SPEED FOR ROCKET

30 YEARS AGO

1949 FIRST STEP ROCKET A MODIFIED GERMAN V2

1. A Russian teacher was the first man to work out that a rocket had to go at 25,000 m.p.h. to leave the earth.

2. An American, Robert Goddard, made rockets with liquid fuel. They did not go very high.

3. Step-rockets can go faster and farther than single rockets. The first step-rocket went as high as 244 miles.

4. The Russians were the first to put a satellite into orbit around the earth. It stayed in space for three months.

5. The first man in space was also a Russian. He was called Yuri Gagarin.

6. The Americans launched a two-manned spacecraft. It was called Gemini.

7. The Russians sent the first rocket all the way to the moon. It crash-landed. It had no people in it.

8. The first instrument to make a soft landing on the moon was Russian. It was called Luna 9. A special rocket stopped it from crashing.

25 YEARS AGO

5 YEARS AGO

1969 FIRST MEN ON THE MOON (NEIL ARMSTRONG AND 'BUZZ' ALDRIN)

1966—1968 SOFT LANDINGS ON MOON — SENT BACK PICTURES TO EARTH

ORBITERS MAPPED THE MOON

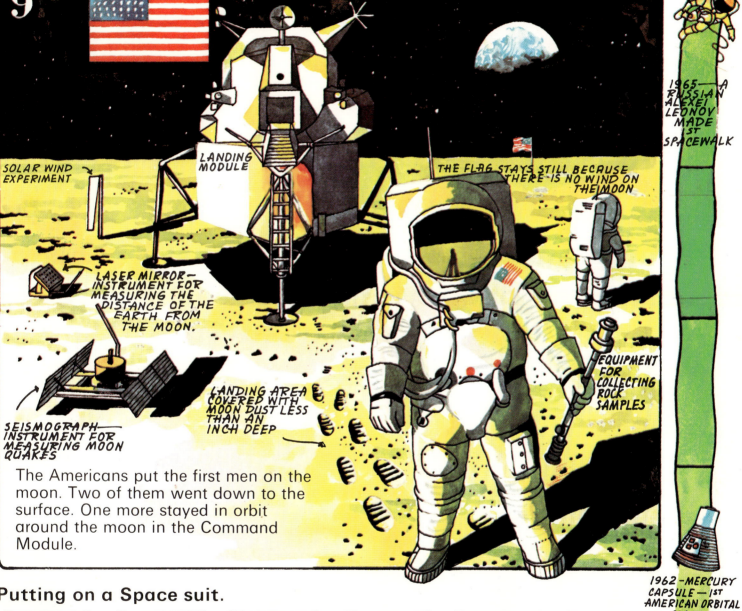

9

SOLAR WIND EXPERIMENT

LANDING MODULE

THE FLAG STAYS STILL BECAUSE THERE IS NO WIND ON THE MOON

LASER MIRROR — INSTRUMENT FOR MEASURING THE DISTANCE OF THE EARTH FROM THE MOON.

SEISMOGRAPH — INSTRUMENT FOR MEASURING MOON QUAKES

LANDING AREA COVERED WITH MOON DUST LESS THAN AN INCH DEEP

EQUIPMENT FOR COLLECTING ROCK SAMPLES

1965 — A RUSSIAN ALEXEI LEONOV MADE 1ST SPACEWALK

The Americans put the first men on the moon. Two of them went down to the surface. One more stayed in orbit around the moon in the Command Module.

Putting on a Space suit.

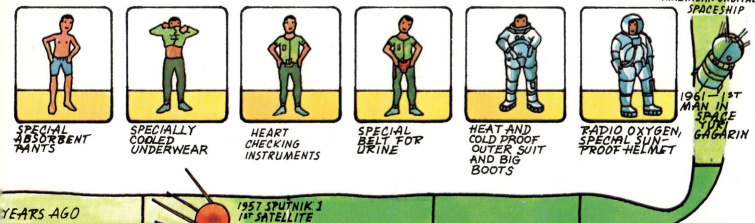

SPECIAL ABSORBENT PANTS

SPECIALLY COOLED UNDERWEAR

HEART CHECKING INSTRUMENTS

SPECIAL BELT FOR URINE

HEAT AND COLD PROOF OUTER SUIT AND BIG BOOTS

RADIO OXYGEN, SPECIAL SUN-PROOF HELMET

1962 — MERCURY CAPSULE — 1ST AMERICAN ORBITAL SPACESHIP

1961 — 1ST MAN IN SPACE YURI GAGARIN

YEARS AGO

1957 SPUTNIK 1 1ST SATELLITE

COLOUR
CARTOON
FILMS

Moving Pictures

300 YEARS AGO

The first cameras took photographs very slowly. These pictures were taken, seconds after each other, with three different cameras. When joined they looked like a film.

Cameras became faster at taking photos. This film was about a fire. It was made when engines were pulled by horses. It had no sound or colour and was very short.

Then two men made a camera which was light enough to carry about. It took photos on rolls of film. People made news films.

These men are working the arms and head of a giant creature. It was used in one of the first French science fiction films.

This was one of the first Hollywood epic films. It was about ancient Babylon and lasted for three-and-a-half hours. Hundreds of people acted in it.

This is a scene from a film about a brave hero who saves the heroine just in time. The stories of early films were very simple and usually had happy endings.

1930
BAIRD'S TELEVISION—
1ST TELEVISION SET
SOLD IN BRITAIN

COMEDY
FILM
STARS

1895,
LUMIERE BROTHER'S
CAMERA WITH ROLLS
OF FILM

1892-3
EDISON/DICKSON
KINETOSCOPE—
1ST PUBLIC
SHOWING

100 YEARS AGO

1877
MUYBRIDGE'S
GALLOPING
HORSE—
1ST ACTION
PICTURES

These are the Keystone Kops. They were in lots of the first comedy films. The film was speeded up to make them seem to move faster.

The first cinemas often used to pay somebody to play the piano during a film. The music became exciting when the film did.

One problem with the first talking pictures, was where to put the microphone. Actors found microphones difficult to use at first.

© Walt Disney Productions

Then people started to make coloured films. Some of the first ones were Mickey Mouse cartoons made by Walt Disney.

The first television sets had a tiny flickering picture. You had to be very close to the screen to see it. Only one person could watch.

This cameraman is working the first electronic camera. It took much better pictures than mechanical cameras.

The picture gets better
The first television pictures were very patchy. Now they are made of so many tiny lines that they look completely clear.

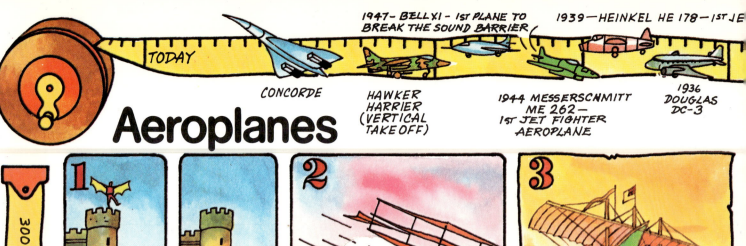

1947— BELL XI — 1ST PLANE TO BREAK THE SOUND BARRIER

1939—HEINKEL HE 178—1ST JE[T]

TODAY

CONCORDE

HAWKER HARRIER (VERTICAL TAKE OFF)

1944 MESSERSCHMITT ME 262— 1ST JET FIGHTER AEROPLANE

1936 DOUGLAS DC-3

Aeroplanes

300 YEARS AGO

At first men tried to fly like birds. But people are too heavy. They are not strong enough to flap big wings.

The first plane that flew with a person in it, had fixed wings. A boy flew a short way in it.

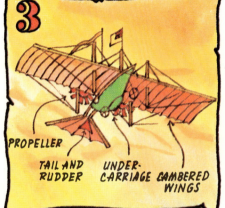

PROPELLER

TAIL AND RUDDER

UNDER-CARRIAGE

CAMBERED WINGS

This was an early plan for a plane with a steam engine. But it could not have worked. Steam engines are much too heavy.

None of these early aeroplanes worked very well.

This glider often flew quite well. But the pilot had to swing his legs to control it. This was very difficult and dangerous.

The first plane to fly properly had a light petrol engine in it. The pilot could bend the wings to control it.

The first proper powered flights were made in America. This aeroplane was one of the first European aeroplanes to fly.

20[0]

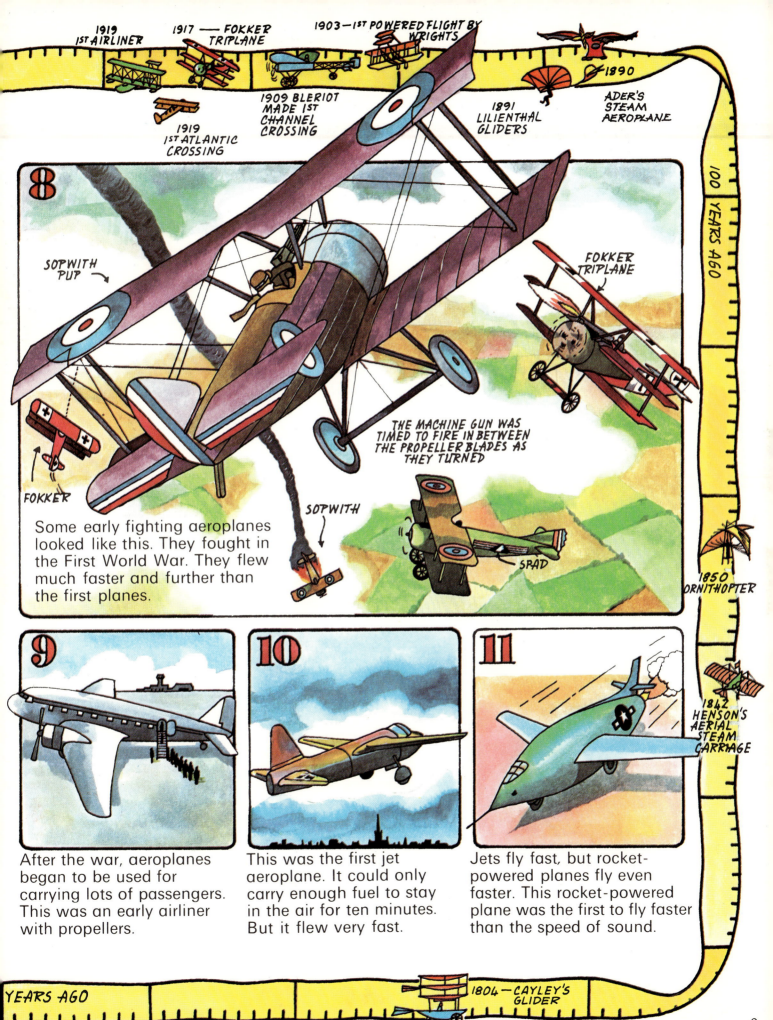

1964 BLUEBIRD-PROTEUS
1ST CAR TO GO OVER
403 m.p.h.

1950
AMERICAN CAR-
CHEVROLET

1943
VOLKSWAGEN

1938
RAILTON
WENT OVER
350 m.p.h.

Cars

300 YEARS AGO

1

A long time ago, there were no cars. The gig was probably the fastest thing on wheels. It could go at about 11 m.p.h. until the horses became tired.

2

The first carriage to move on its own had a steam engine. It could only go at 3 m.p.h. The steering-handle was so stiff, only a strong man could turn it.

3

This steam bus could go at 12 m.p.h. But it needed an awful lot of water. It could only go a short way before it had to stop for some more.

4

THE WHEELS HAD HARD OR METAL EDGES. THIS CAR WAS BUMPY TO RIDE IN.

A STEERING HANDLE → TURNED THE FRONT WHEEL.

This was the first car with a petrol engine. The engine was behind the seat. Petrol engines are lighter than steam engines. But this car could only go at 9 m.p.h. It could not go up hill at all.

THERE WERE ALMOST NO REALLY SMOOTH ROADS IN THOSE DAYS. THE BEST ROADS USUALLY HAD COBBLE STONES ON THEM.

1769
NICHOLAS CUGNOT -
STEAM CARRIAGE
1ST

1927
SUNBEAM
1ST CAR TO GO
OVER 203 M.P.H.

1915 FORD

1908
1ST MODEL T
FORD

1904 DARRACQ
1ST CAR TO GO
OVER 104 M.P.H.

1898
1ST RENAULT

1891 PANHARD-
LEVASSOR. 1ST
CAR WITH GEARS

1886 DAIMLER
1ST 4-WHEELED
CAR

1885
KARL BENZ
1ST CAR

1873.
AMÉDÉE
BOLLÉE
STEAM
BUS

This was a safer car because it had four wheels. But it was still very slow. It could only go at 10 m.p.h.

This car was much faster because it had 3 gears for different speeds. It could go at 18 m.p.h. in top gear.

People quickly learnt how to make really fast cars with enormous engines. This old racing car could go at 104 m.p.h.

As cars got faster, policemen had to stop people driving at dangerous speeds. In 1904, you were not allowed to drive faster than 20 m.p.h.

The first cars were very expensive. Then Ford cars were made. They were the first cars lots of people could afford to buy.

Motoring Long Ago

YOU HAD TO TURN A STIFF HANDLE TO START. THIS COULD BE DANGEROUS.

THE WATER IN THE RADIATOR OFTEN BOILED OVER.

IF YOU WENT TOO FAST FOR TOO LONG, THE ENGINE SOMETIMES BLEW UP.

MOST ROADS WERE DREADFULLY DUSTY.

CARS HAD TO BE TALL ENOUGH FOR LADIES WITH BIG HATS.

YOU GOT PETROL FROM CHEMISTS AND IRONMONGERS. BLACKSMITHS USUALLY DID REPAIRS.

1831
STEAM
COACH

200 YEARS AGO

1803 RICHARD TREVITHICK 1ST STEAM COACH

1960 — HONDA, JAPANESE MACHINES
BECOME POPULAR ON WORLD MARKET

1939 — GERMAN
MOTORBIKE USED
IN THE SECOND
WORLD WAR

Bicycles

300 YEARS AGO

1 The first bicycle was a sort of hobby-horse on wheels. It had no pedals so you had to push it forward like a scooter. It was impossible to steer.

2 You could steer this bicycle by turning the handle-bars. But you still had to push it along with your feet.

3 This was one of the first bicycles with pedals. Pedalling was very hard work. The pedals went backwards and forwards and drove the back wheel.

4 The next bicycle had pedals that went round. It was so much better that lots of people bought bicycles. These men even went to a bicycle-riding school to learn how to ride properly. But the bicycles were so uncomfortable to sit on they were called bone shakers.

5 Then people discovered that bicycles with very big front wheels went faster. These were called penny farthings. It was easy to fall off them.

GETTING ON AT FIRST

WHEN YOU GET BETTER

GOING DOWN HILL

GETTING OFF

ANOTHER WAY TO GET OFF

AND ANOTHER WAY

1926 B.M.W.

1917—TRIUMPH USED IN THE FIRST WORLD WAR

1911 INDIAN

DE DION BOUTON MOTOR TRICYCLE 1898

PETROL-ENGINED MOTOR BIKE 1891

SAFETY BICYCLE

1870 PENNY FARTHING

1868—1st MOTORCYCLE

1861 BONESHAKER

One man rode all the way round the world on a penny farthing. He kept it in a tent at night.

Some of the first tricycles were for two people.

This was one of the first motorcycle side-cars.

This old tricycle had a small wheel at the back.

Some people did not like the first cyclists. They set traps for them.

6

This was the first bicycle which was safe and fast. The pedals drove the back wheel by a chain.

1 Motorcycles

The first motorcycle was a boneshaker driven by a tiny steam engine. It had iron tyres and no brakes.

2

This was one of the first motorcycles with a petrol engine. It managed to go at 24 m.p.h.

1839 MACMILLAN'S CYCLE—1st BICYCLE WITH PEDALS

YEARS AGO

1791 DE SIVRAC'S BICYCLE—1st BICYCLE

1817 KARL VON DRAIS BICYCLE—1st ONE WITH HANDLE BARS

Cameras and Photographs

Before there were cameras, only a few people had enough money to have their portraits painted. There were even fewer people who could paint.

People who were not very good at painting could trace a view with a camera obscura. They traced a reflection of the view from the top bit of glass.

This was the first camera which took photos on paper. You could make several copies of each picture.

Later there was another kind of camera. Its photographs were not made on paper, but on metal. You only got one copy of each picture.

It took a long time to take a photograph. People had to sit still all this time. They had clamps round their heads to stop them moving.

Early photographers had to take a lot of things with them. This was because they wet the glass photo-plate before they could take a picture. As people

thought up new ways to take photographs, the photographer's load became lighter. All he needed fitted into a suitcase.

1889
DETECTIVE
CAMERA

1889
KODAK
1ST ROLL FILM
CAMERA

1885
PHOTOGRAPHIC
GUN

100 YEARS AGO

1861
1ST ATTEMPTS
AT COLOUR
PHOTOGRAPHY

1851
WET PLATE
PHOTOS

1840
DAGUERREOTYPE
PHOTOS

1835
FOX TALBOT
1ST CAMERA

1825
1ST PHOTO

6

Kodak cameras were the first to have rolls of film inside. This made taking pictures much easier. You just pressed a button and wound the film on.

Some cameras looked very odd. This one was called a Photographic Gun.

This man is taking a picture with a hidden detective camera under his waistcoat.

You needed very bright light to take a picture indoors. Photographers made a flash by burning magnesium.

Often the photographer's flash went wrong and covered everybody with soot.

CAMERA OBSCURA

Trains

CANADIAN TURBOTRAIN

1960 ELECTRIC TRAIN

1956 SKYWAY MONORAIL

STANDARD 9 — LAST STEAM LOCOMOTIVE BUILT FOR BRITISH RAILWAYS

300 YEARS AGO

1

Rails were invented before railway engines. Horses often pulled wagons up hill and followed behind on the way down.

2

This was one of the first railway engines. It had a steam engine. But it was very slow and took a very long time to get up steam.

COKE MADE LESS SMOKE THAN COAL.

3

A BARREL WITH SPARE WATER

MAN STOKING FIRE WITH COKE

STEAM PUSHED THIS PUMP UP AND DOWN. THE PUMP MADE THE WHEELS GO ROUND

ROCKET

Robert Stephenson's Rocket was a much faster railway engine. It was the first train to go faster than 35 m.p.h.

It was one of the first engines with springs. Without springs, it could have been shaken apart at speed. It had a new sort of

boiler, which heated water up much more quickly. This meant that the engine did not take long to start.

1935
STREAMLINED
LOCOMOTIVE

1923 - A GREAT
WESTERN CASTLE
CLASS LOCOMOTIVE

SUSPENSION
RAILWAY

1ST CLASS
CARRIAGE

1879
WERNER VON
SIEMEN'S
ELECTRIC
TRAIN

4

Some trains made much more smoke. This American train made so much smoke and so many sparks the passengers' clothes caught fire.

5

Building railways through Indian territory in America could be dangerous. The Indians tried to stop the railwaymen.

1869—UNION PACIFIC RAILWAY OPENED

2ND CLASS CARRIAGES

1865 1ST SLEEPING CAR

1863—1ST UNDERGROUND

At first, second class railway carriages were open, with holes in the floor to let rain run out. First class passengers were more comfortable.

6

These men are building the first underground. They dug up whole streets, laid the track and made the tunnels. Then they put the streets back on top again.

7

The first trains in the London underground had steam engines and open carriages. People got very dirty when they travelled.

Railway lines had to be almost level, because it was difficult for trains to go up and down hills. So the men who built the railways made cuttings and tunnels in hills. They made viaducts and bridges over valleys and rivers.

1831 DE WITT CLINTON

1830—TOM THUMB 1ST AMERICAN TRAIN

1829 STEPHENSON'S ROCKET

Making the Track Level

YEARS AGO

1808 - CATCH-ME-WHO-CAN

1825-LOCOMOTION No1 1ST STEAM PASSENGER TRAIN

1813 - PUFFING BILLY

17

1960 - HIGH
ALTITUDE
BALLOON

1929 - GRAF ZEPPELIN LZ-127
PASSENGER AIRSHIP
MADE FLIGHT AROUND THE WOR

Balloons

300 YEARS AGO

1

These animals were the first air passengers. They flew for eight minutes in a hot air balloon that was as high as a three-storey house.

2

The first human balloonists could control their balloon a bit. They made it go up by making the fire burn fiercely and down by dampening it.

3

Another balloon was the hydrogen gas balloon. It went higher if it had a lot of gas in it. This is how people filled it with gas.

5

People used balloons for lots of different things. These men went up in this balloon to see what the enemy was doing. They put messages in bags and lowered them down ropes to the soldiers below. Lots of men held the ropes to keep the balloon steady and stop it from blowing away.

6

Balloons only go where the wind blows them. Airships are balloons with engines. This one could turn corners and fly against the wind.

Sometimes balloons were blown miles off course. These men had to walk for days after landing in ice and snow.

209

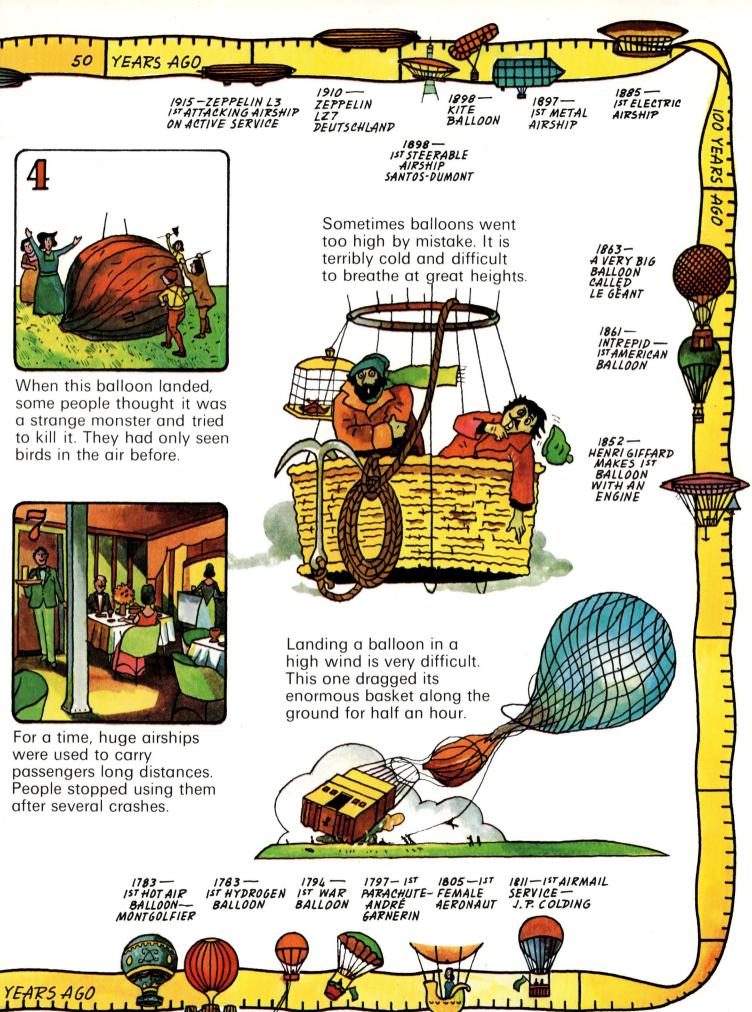

1915 — ZEPPELIN L3
1ST ATTACKING AIRSHIP
ON ACTIVE SERVICE

1910 —
ZEPPELIN
LZ7
DEUTSCHLAND

1898 —
KITE
BALLOON

1897 —
1ST METAL
AIRSHIP

1885 —
1ST ELECTRIC
AIRSHIP

1898 —
1ST STEERABLE
AIRSHIP
SANTOS-DUMONT

100 YEARS AGO

4

When this balloon landed, some people thought it was a strange monster and tried to kill it. They had only seen birds in the air before.

Sometimes balloons went too high by mistake. It is terribly cold and difficult to breathe at great heights.

1863 —
A VERY BIG
BALLOON
CALLED
LE GÉANT

1861 —
INTREPID —
1ST AMERICAN
BALLOON

1852 —
HENRI GIFFARD
MAKES 1ST
BALLOON
WITH AN
ENGINE

7

For a time, huge airships were used to carry passengers long distances. People stopped using them after several crashes.

Landing a balloon in a high wind is very difficult. This one dragged its enormous basket along the ground for half an hour.

1783 —
1ST HOT AIR
BALLOON —
MONTGOLFIER

1783 —
1ST HYDROGEN
BALLOON

1794 —
1ST WAR
BALLOON

1797 — 1ST
PARACHUTE —
ANDRÉ
GARNERIN

1805 — 1ST
FEMALE
AERONAUT

1811 — 1ST AIRMAIL
SERVICE —
J. P. COLDING

YEARS AGO

Message Machines

300 YEARS AGO

Before message-sending machines were invented, people sent signals with drums, smoke, fires, huge horns, church bells and flashing mirrors.

This was one of the first message machines. It was called the Semaphore. The arms made a special sign for each letter. Semaphore stations were on the top of hills. They took a message and then sent it on to the next station, letter by letter. Messages travelled 90 times faster than men on horseback could carry them.

The Shutter Telegraph was another kind of message machine. You worked it by opening and shutting one of the shutters.

One of the first electric telegraph machines sent electric currents along wires. The current made needles point to different letters.

TRAIN ATTACKED BY INDIANS

YOUR MESSAGE SAYS, 'TRAIN ATTACKED BY INDIANS'

Samuel Morse invented a code for telegraph messages. The sender tapped out different sets of dots and dashes for each letter. At the other end of the wire, a decoder turned the dots and dashes back into letters and words.

200

50 YEARS AGO

1ST WIRELESS PROGRAMMES

1901 – 1ST TRANSATLANTIC WIRELESS SIGNAL

1894 – 1ST SEMI-AUTOMATIC SWITCHBOARD

1878 – 1ST SWITCHBOARD

1876 – 1ST TELEPHONE INVENTED BY ALEXANDER BELL

1866 – 1ST SUCCESSFUL UNDERWATER TRANSATLANTIC CABLE

1846 – TELEGRAPH THAT PRINTS LETTERS INVENTED

1843 – MORSE CODE TELEGRAPH

1837 – ELECTRIC TELEGRAPH

6

The telephone turned the sound of a voice into electric currents. It turned the currents back into voice sounds at the other end of the line.

7

HELLO – NUMBER PLEASE

SORRY CALLER, I CAN'T HEAR YOU

CAN YOU REPEAT THAT NUMBER

HELLO

HOLD ON I HAVE A CALL FOR YOU

Girls at telephone switchboards joined different lines together by hand. You always had to ask the operator for the number you wanted. Once automatic switchboards were invented, you could dial your number without the help of an operator.

8

The wireless worked without any wires. It sends radio waves through space from one wireless set to another. This ship has sent a wireless message to the lighthouse to call for help.

9

Nowadays space satellites help send radio, television and telephone messages further and more clearly.

1793 – SEMAPHORE

1795 – SHUTTER TELEGRAPH

YEARS AGO

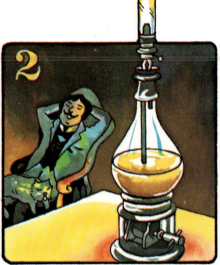

Lighting

Indoor Lights

SHELL LAMP

SAUCER LAMP

ROMAN LAMPS

CANDLES

1500 SNUFFERS

300 YEARS AGO

Before electric lights and switches, people lit their homes with candles and oil lamps. These did not give off much light.

People could not leave a candle to burn on its own. They had to cut the wick off every half an hour to stop it smelling nasty.

Then somebody invented a new kind of oil lamp which was much brighter. People did not need to get up all the time to trim its wick.

The first gas lights were just holes in iron pipes. The pipes came into each room from outside.

Later gas pipes were led into specially made lamps.

Gas lighting was even brighter than electric lighting when gas lamps had something called a mantle fixed on to them.

The first electric lamp looked a bit like a glass banana with a thread inside it. This thread became so hot when electricity went through it that it shone.

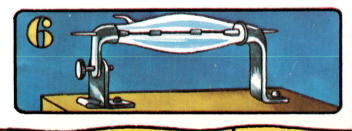

FLINT MILL

EARLY ATTEMPTS AT NEON LIGHTING

RAILWAY READING LAMPS

GAS LAMPS

ELECTRIC SAFETY LAMPS

1878 — ELECTRIC INDOOR LAMPS

1859 — PARAFFIN LAMPS

STAGE LIGHTING

Street Lights

A long time ago, there were no street lamps. It was so dark at night you had to carry a lantern. It was dangerous to be out.

Gas lights made the streets much brighter and safer. This man was a lamp lighter. His job was to go from lamp to lamp turning the gas on and lighting it.

These were the first electric street lamps. They are called arc lamps. Even though they were very bright, gas street lights were used more often.

Lights in Coalmines

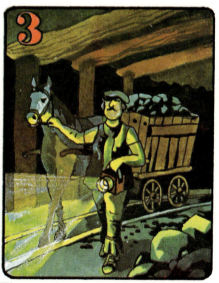

It is very dangerous for miners to take candles and oil lamps into mines. Before gas and electric lamps, a machine like this was often their only light.

This was a special sort of oil lamp. The flame in it was covered so that it would be safer than a candle. It was a sort of warning lamp as well.

Then miners carried electric lamps down in the mines. These were much safer.

BETTER CANDLEWICKS

1784 CARCEL OIL LAMP

1792 — EARLY ATTEMPTS AT GAS LIGHTING

1807 — 1ST STREET GAS LIGHTING

MINER'S OIL SAFETY LAMP

1841—1ST ELECTRIC CLOCK

POCKET WATCHES

GRAN CLOC

EARLY WATCHES

1656 PENDULUM CLOCK

TODAY

Telling the Time

1 A long time ago, there were no mechanical clocks. These people are watching a shadow move round a stone to tell them the hour. Maybe this was the first sundial.

2 They might have used another sort of shadow clock, like this one.

3 They might have had a water clock, like this. As water dripped out of it, the level went down from one mark to the next, showing the time.

4 Then people made sundials out of blocks of stone. This one had a metal rod sticking out of it, called a gnomon. The gnomon cast a shadow on an hour mark.

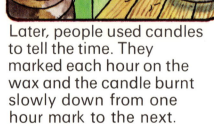

5 Later, people used candles to tell the time. They marked each hour on the wax and the candle burnt slowly down from one hour mark to the next.

6 People used sand glasses too. Sailors hung them on their ships. When the ship heeled over, the sand glass always stayed upright.

This is how the first alarm clock may have worked.

3000 YEARS AGO

SUNDIAL SHADOW CLOCK

SHADOW CLOCK

WATER CLOCK

300 B.C. ROMAN SUNDIAL

CANDLE CLOCK

7

This man's job was to wind up the weights of this old turret clock. It was hard work, because the weights often reached the ground.

The first clocks were not very accurate. People had to check their clocks against sundials.

At first mechanical clocks had no hands. Then some of them had just one, to point out the hour. Some clocks were calendars too. Others had puppet figures.

This man was very proud of his clock. He decided to have his portrait painted with the clock in the picture as well.

8

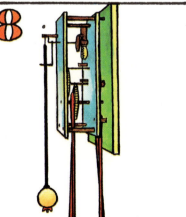

Clocks only became accurate when pendulum clocks were invented. The pendulum swung to and fro very regularly. Clocks began to have two hands.

Clockmakers formed a guild. Sometimes they seized and broke up badly-made clocks.

Printing

1814 — 1ST STEAM DRIVEN PRESS

3000 YEARS AGO

2000

2 THE PAPER-MAKER PUT THE PAPER BETWEEN PIECES OF FELT TO DRY.

The pictures on the top half of these two pages show you how people used to make paper and print on it. At the bottom, you can see inventions that made paper-making and printing much faster.

THE PAPER-MAKER PUT THE PILE OF PAPER AND FELT IN A PAPER PRESS.

3 THE PAPER PRESS SQUASHED THE PILE TO MAKE THE PAPER SMOOTH.

THIS BARREL IS FULL OF A WATERY MIXTURE OF LINEN OR COTTON FIBRES MADE OF RAGS. PAPER-MAKERS DIPPED A SIEVE-LIKE TRAY TO SPREAD THE FIBRES OUT EVENLY TO MAKE A SHEET OF PAPER.

1

THE PAPER-MAKER TOOK THE FELT AWAY. THEN THE PAPER WAS COMPLETELY DRIED BEFORE IT WAS SENT TO THE PRINTER.

4

Paper-Making Machines

PULP VAT

PULP FIBRE

SMOOTHING ROLLERS

ROLL OF FINISHED PAPER

WATER IS DRAINED OUT

This is a paper-making machine. You no longer had to make paper one sheet at a time. The machine made a whole reel in one go.

Composing Machines

This machine could make letters into words and lines much more quickly than a man could. It was called a Linotype machine.

1450—1ST PRINTING PRESSES WITH MOVABLE TYPE

1150—1ST PAPER MILL IN EUROPE

1041 TYPE INVENTED IN CHINA

WOODBLOCK PRINTING MADE IN CHINA

7

THE PRINTER DABBED THE LETTERS WITH INK-COVERED LEATHER BALLS.

6 THEN THE PRINTER LOCKED A WHOLE PAGE OF LETTERS INTO A FRAME CALLED A FORME.

8 THE PRINTER PRESSED THE PAPER AND FORME TOGETHER TO PRINT THE PAPER. THE PRINTING PRESS OFTEN PRINTED HALF A SHEET OF PAPER AT A TIME.

9 THE PRINTER HUNG UP PRINTED SHEETS OF PAPER TO DRY.

5 THIS MAN PUT LETTERS ONE BY ONE INTO A PIECE OF WOOD CALLED A COMPOSING STICK. HE WAS CALLED A COMPOSITOR.

1 Printing Machines

PAPER FED IN HERE

PAPER BEING FED IN

This machine could print flat sheets of paper much quicker than the old presses.

Men only had to get the machine ready, put the paper in and let the machine do the rest.

2

PRINTED PAPER

TYPE ROLLER

INKING ROLLER

BIG ROLL OF PAPER

This machine prints even faster. It prints whole rolls of paper and cuts them into sheets later.

SUNKEN BATH

1889 – 1ST WASHDOWN LAVATORY

MODERN LAVATORY

RAIN BATH SHOWER

FRENCH BATH CALLED DEMI-BAIN

1778 – BRAMAH LAVATORY

BATH SPA

CLOSED STOOL

Keeping Clean

3000 YEARS AGO

1ST BATHS

500 B.C. ROMAN BATHS

1 Baths

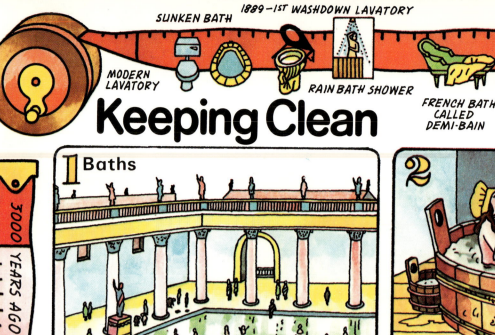

A long time ago in Rome and Crete, people built marvellous baths. Some of them even had hot and cold running water. This huge bath was public. Everybody could use it.

2

This bath had to be filled with hot water by hand. It took 30 gallons to fill. The people in it ate meals at the same time as they had their baths.

3

This place had special water. People went bathing there when they felt unwell.

As it took such a long time to fill a bath tub, they did not have baths at home very often.

4

But some people were frightened of getting wet because they had taken so few baths. This lady screamed and struggled when she had her first shower.

200

1596 —
HARINGTON'S
LAVATORY

1090 —
MEDIEVAL
BATH

1000 YEARS AGO

5

After thousands of years, running water began to be used in homes again. This bath had a shower and hot and cold water at the turn of a tap.

1 Lavatories

Towns were very smelly and unhealthy places before there were flushing lavatories. People used to empty their slops into the street below.

2

If you were rich, you might have used something like this. When you had finished, you just closed the lid and somebody else emptied it for you.

3

This was one of the first lavatories. You turned the brown knob to flush everything into a pit below. But somebody still had to empty the pit later.

4

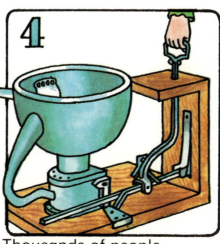

Thousands of people bought this lavatory. If you pulled the handle up, two flaps opened. One let the water in and the other let it drain away.

5

This was one of the first lavatories which you flushed by pulling the chain. It made a terrible noise as water streamed from the cistern above.

Money

1793
1ST AMERICAN
COINS MADE

1661
1ST PAPER MONEY
IN EUROPE
(SWEDEN)

TOOLS

CHUNKS OF
SILVER
USED AS
MONEY

JEWELLERY
USED AS
MONEY

BRONZE
BAR
SHAPED
LIKE AN
OX-HIDE

690 B.C.
1ST COIN
(LYDIA)

550 B.C.
1ST GOLD
AND
SILVER
COINS

1

A long time ago, there were no shops. If you needed an axe, you would probably have had to make it yourself. Then, if you made many axes, you could swop one for something else you needed. This is called barter.

Barter did not always work. The man swopped his axe for the apples he needed. But, the other man still had many apples. If nobody needed them, they would go bad and he would never be able to swop them for other things.

2

People started to use as money all sorts of things which would not go bad. They used such things as flint spear heads, axe heads, cowrie shells, whales' teeth, metal bracelets and gold necklaces.

3

Then people began to make things to be used only as money. Some of the first metal money that we know about looked like cow skins. Perhaps each bit was worth a cow.

4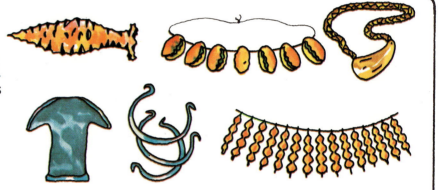

Then people started making coins. They were much easier to carry. Coins often had pictures of gods and kings on them to make them seem important.

GREEK TETRADRACHM THOUGHT TO BE THE MOST BEAUTIFUL COIN IN THE WORLD

300 B.C. ROMAN COIN WITH A COW ON IT

2000 YEA

500 YEARS AGO

1ST BANKS (ITALY)

1300 — MINT AT TOWER OF LONDON OPENED. MADE COINS FOR CENTURIES.

1000 YEARS AGO

Making Coins

These men made coins in a mint. First they melted the metal in a furnace (a). Then they bashed it to make it thin and flat (b). Then they cut it into coin shapes (c). Lastly they stamped both sides with a picture (d).

1 Banking

Before there were banks, people had to look after their money themselves. This man hid his money in the safest place that he could find.

If this did not work, he had to find somewhere else to put his money. He probably put it in the safest place in town, which was the goldsmith's shop.

Lots of people started taking their money to the goldsmith's shop. The goldsmith locked it away safely. These shops became the first banks.

The goldsmith wrote the amount of money he had been given on a piece of paper. He gave the paper to the owner of the money. This became a bank note.

Catching out a Crook

This crook chipped bits of metal off the edge of coins and nobody knew. But when people made coins with tiny dents around the edge, he had to stop. It was easy to see if a coin was chipped.

The crook tried forging bank notes. But the pattern on the note was very complicated and difficult for him to copy. It was quite easy to spot that the note was not real.

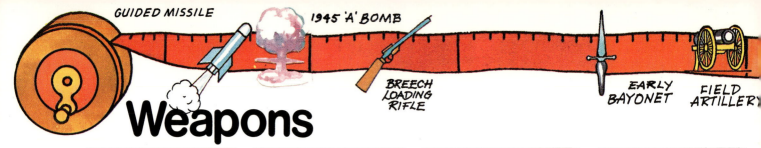
Weapons

1 A long time ago, people probably fought with their fists or with clubs and stones. You can still see some of their simple weapons in museums.

Then men learnt to sharpen bits of flintstone to make spears, axes and knives. They also used slings and flint-tipped arrows.

CLUBS

STONES

SHARPENED STONES

AXES

WOODEN JAVELINS

SWORDS

DAGGERS

JAVELIN WITH METAL HEAD

BOWS AND ARROWS

2 A SOLDIER WITH A SLING WOULD SWING IT ROUND HIS HEAD VERY FAST. THEN HE WOULD LET ONE STRAP GO AND A LEAD PELLET WOULD SHOOT AWAY AT GREAT SPEED.

ROMAN SOLDIERS FOUGHT IN GROUPS CALLED LEGIONS. EACH LEGION HAD A STANDARD.

SHIELD MADE OF LAYERS OF WOOD.

THE JAVELIN TOOK A LONG TIME TO LEARN HOW TO THROW AND YOU HAD TO BE VERY STRONG. EACH SOLDIER HAD TWO.

METAL HELMET

ARMOUR MADE OF STRIPS OF METAL JOINED TOGETHER.

LEATHER TUNIC

For thousands of years, soldiers fought mainly with metal spears, swords and arrow tips. They had shields and armour to protect them.

1 One of the most powerful bows ever made was the English long bow. Only very strong, well-trained soldiers could use it. It could shoot arrows 150 metres.

2 The cross bow was a very powerful bow too. It could be used by soldiers who had no special training.

3 To re-load a cross bow you had to wind it up with handles. This made the cross bow slower to shoot than the long bow.

3000   YEARS AGO   20

SLING

SPANISH MUSKET   HEAVY STEEL CROSS BOW   1400 EARLY HAND GUN   EARLY CANNONS   LONG BOW   CROSS BOW

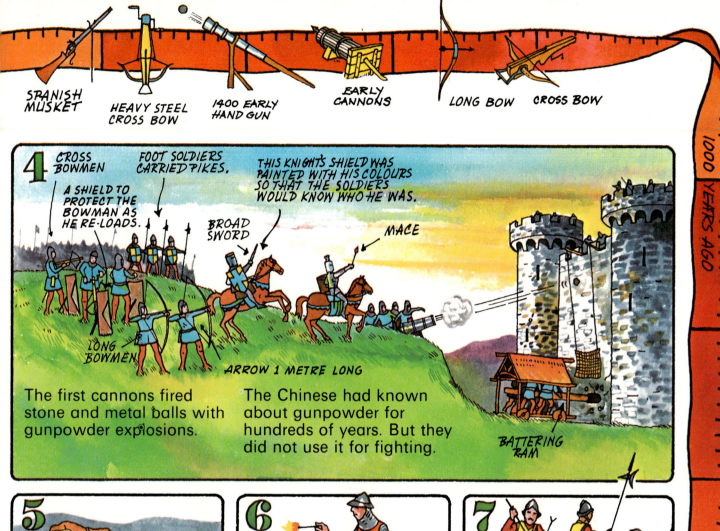

4
CROSS BOWMEN

A SHIELD TO PROTECT THE BOWMAN AS HE RE-LOADS.

FOOT SOLDIERS CARRIED PIKES.

THIS KNIGHT'S SHIELD WAS PAINTED WITH HIS COLOURS SO THAT THE SOLDIERS WOULD KNOW WHO HE WAS.

BROAD SWORD

MACE

LONG BOWMEN

ARROW 1 METRE LONG

BATTERING RAM

The first cannons fired stone and metal balls with gunpowder explosions.

The Chinese had known about gunpowder for hundreds of years. But they did not use it for fighting.

5 Cannons were very heavy. It took a long time to move them from one place to another. They often got stuck in the mud.

6 The first hand-guns were very difficult to fire. You had to load them down the barrel. Then you had to hold them steady while you touched them off.

7 These guns were easier to fire. They had a trigger. But soldiers still loaded them down the barrel. They had pikemen to protect them as they loaded.

8 Guns became more accurate when people cut tiny grooves inside the barrel. These grooves made the bullet spin. This was called rifling.

9 Firing became quicker when guns opened at the breech. Soldiers did not have to push the bullet and powder all the way down the barrel anymore.

10 Then came a new kind of gun. It used cartridges, which contain both bullets and powder. Soldiers could fire many cartridges without having to re-load.

Castles

1

RAMPARTS OF EARTH

CHIEF'S HUT

CORN WAS KEPT HERE

CHIEF'S CHARIOT

WAR TRUMPET

THESE MEN OPENED AND SHUT THE GATES

THORNY HEDGE

FENCED VILLAGE

1000 B.C. VERY SIMPLE HILL FORT

The first castles were probably just villages surrounded by a wooden fence. People usually built them on top of a hill, so that they would be able to see what was going on around them. This Celtic hill-fort had deep ditches and huge ramparts of earth around it. Some of these were over 26 metres high.

2

One of the problems with wooden walls was that if the enemy could get close enough, they could set fire to them.

3

Stone castles with battlements were safer. But attackers could still get in by climbing up the walls on scaling ladders.

4

Even castles with high walls were not safe. Attackers could dig a tunnel under a wall, keep it up with props, set fire to them and make the wall fall down.

300 B.C. HILL FORT

200

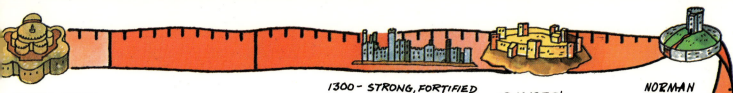

NORMAN WOOD CASTLE

5

The weakest part of an outer wall was its corner. This was the easiest place for attackers to knock holes with a battering ram and get in.

Defenders who wanted to attack soldiers right at the base of a castle had to lean right over the parapet. This made them very easy to shoot.

6

Once the enemy had knocked down the outer wall, the castle had to surrender. This was because all the stores and animals were kept in the courtyard.

7

ATTACKERS SURROUNDED THE CASTLE SO THAT NO FOOD COULD GET IN.

ARROW SLITS WERE SO NARROW THAT IT WAS DIFFICULT FOR ENEMY ARROWS TO GO THROUGH THEM.

MOAT FILLED WITH WATER

HOLES FOR SHOOTING ARROWS OUT OF AND FOR DROPPING HEAVY STICKS AND HOT TAR OR BOILING OIL ON ATTACKERS.

BARBICAN

SPIKY PORTCULLIS

THE CASTLE HAD A DOUBLE DOOR WITH HINGES ON THE INSIDE SO THAT ATTACKERS COULD NOT TAKE THE DOOR OFF.

THE MOAT HAS BEEN FILLED IN TO ALLOW THE SIEGE TOWER AND SCALING LADDERS TO BE USED.

This castle had a moat and high, round towers. It had very high, thick walls to protect it against battering rams and siege towers. The wooden hoardings on the walls made it safer for defenders when they attacked enemy soldiers below. Attackers hardly ever got past the gatehouse. But when gunpowder and cannons were invented, castle walls could be knocked down more easily.

1898 – 1ST SUBMARINE TO GO INTO OPEN WATER

MAN-OF-WAR

1807 – 1ST PADDLE BOAT SERVICE

1959 1ST HOVERCRAFT

1845 1ST CLIPPER

1843 – FIRST SHIP WITH A PROPELLER TO CROSS ATLANTIC

Boats and Ships ~ 1

LOG BOAT

1ST RAFT

HOLLOWED OUT LOG BOAT

BLOWN UP ANIMAL SKIN BOAT

4,000 B.C. EGYPTIAN BOAT MADE OF REEDS

2500 B.C. CHINESE JUNK

1500 B.C. WARSHIP WITH RAM

1320 B.C. PHOENICIAN SHIPS SAILED TO AFRICA

The first boat was probably just a log. Logs do not make very good boats, because they roll over easily. Somebody must have tied a few logs together to make something too wide to tip up. This was the first raft.

Then men learnt to hollow logs out with axes and fire to make canoes. Other men blew up animal skins and rode on them.

To make warships go faster, builders sometimes made them with two, or even three rows of oars.

The Vikings sailed in cold and stormy seas. Their long, fast ships had high sides to keep the waves out.

The sails were made of leather and often dyed red. Painted shields were hung along the ships' sides.

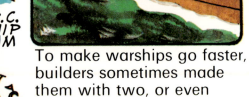

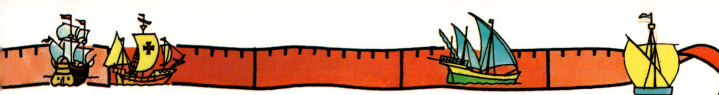

2

3

4

The Ancient Egyptians, who did not have many trees, made boats out of bundles of reeds. They had a sail, so that the wind could blow the boat along.

The first warships we know about looked like this. They had lots of men to row them. They had a pointed ram to make holes in enemy ships.

Early cargo ships had more room in them than the long and narrow warships. They used their sails more than the warships did.

7

8

Most early ships were steered by steering oars at the back and at the sides of the ship. The invention of the rudder at the stern made steering much easier.

Then people built ships with more than one mast and many more smaller sails. Sailors found it easier to move the smaller, lighter sails. The ships went much faster. They went on great voyages around the world.

YEARS AGO

1898 — 1ST SUBMARINE TO GO INTO OPEN WATER

MAN-OF-WAR

1807 — 1ST PADDLE BOAT SERVICE

1959 1ST HOVERCRAFT

1845 1ST CLIPPER

1843 — FIRST SHIP WITH A PROPELLER TO CROSS ATLANTIC

1775 — 1ST SUBMARINE ON ACTIVE SERVICE

Boats and Ships ~ 2

9

POLE TO RAM INTO CANNON

RAT LINES FOR CLIMBING UP TO SAILS →

SHARPSHOOTER

SAILORS TAKING DOWN THEIR HAMMOCKS TO MAKE MORE ROOM FOR FIGHTING

TORCH FOR LIGHTING GUNPOWDER

CANNON BALLS

WATER BUCKET

This is the inside of a fighting ship called a Man-of-War. Cannons were fired through holes in the sides.

LOG BOAT

1ST RAFT

HOLLOWED OUT LOG BOAT

BLOWN UP ANIMAL SKIN BOAT

4,000 B.C. EGYPTIAN BOAT MADE OF REEDS

2500 B.C. CHINESE JUNK

1500 B.C. WARSHIP WITH RAM

1320 B.C. PHOENICIAN SHIPS SAILED TO AFRICA

10

Some of the fastest sailing ships that were ever made, were called 'clippers'. Each year they raced from China to America and Britain.

Captains who sailed very fast arrived with their cargo of tea still fresh. It could be sold for a high price.

11

The first boats with engines were paddle boats. The engine drove the paddles. This kind of paddle boat was used on the Mississippi.

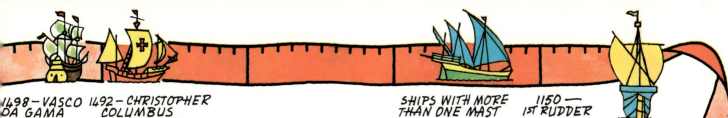
1000 YEARS AGO

800 VIKING SHIP

12

When propellers were first invented, people could not believe they worked as well as paddles. They held a tug-of-war. The boat with a propeller won.

13

Ship builders discovered that ships could be made out of metal. The first metal ocean liner looked like this. It had a steam engine and masts with sails, in case it ran out of fuel. Metal ships could be built much bigger than wooden ships. They were also cheaper to build.

Making Metal Boats

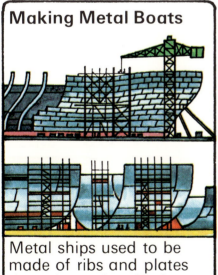

Metal ships used to be made of ribs and plates riveted together. Today whole sections are built separately and then joined.

An Underwater Boat

One of the first submarines was wooden. There was only room for one man inside it. He had to wind a propeller to make the submarine move forward.

Hovercraft

Hovercraft ride on a cushion of air just above the surface of the sea. They can go up on the beach too.

YEARS AGO

1960
FELT-TIPPED PEN

1944 1ST BALL POINT PEN

1884 1ST FOUNTAIN PEN

Writing

INDIAN ROCK DRAWING

3100 B.C. CUNEIFORM WRITING

3100 B.C. CLAY TABLETS

1500 B.C. EGYPTIAN HIEROGLYPHS

1300 B.C. CHINESE WRITING

1200 B.C. STYLUS ON WAX

1170 B.C. FIRST ALPHABET

Pictures and Letters

1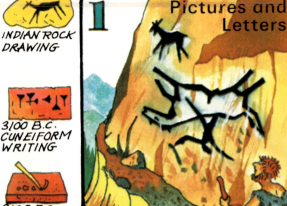

A long time ago, there was no alphabet. People used pictures to leave messages. This old picture message says 'Path safe for goats, not safe for horse-riders'.

2

This picture tells how a man killed five sheep.

3

Then somebody thought of drawing a picture for each word. Can you read 'Man—killed—sheep—five'?

4

The trouble with this idea is that there are too many words. You had to learn a picture for each one. It was too difficult to remember.

5

But suppose you make pictures for sounds, and then join them to make words. You do not need so many pictures.

6

The first letters were really sound pictures drawn very quickly and simply.

Here is some of the First Writing

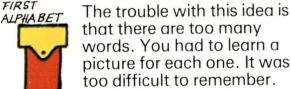

SUMERIAN

CHINESE

PHOENICIAN

EGYPTIAN

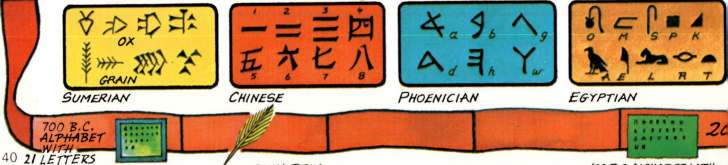

700 B.C. ALPHABET WITH 21 LETTERS

QUILL PENS

100 B.C. ALPHABET WITH 23 LETTERS

40

1000 A.D
ALPHABET WITH
26 LETTERS

1000 YEARS AGO

1 Pens

Before there were pens, people used fingers to make lines. They had no ink, so they sometimes used blood.

Then people stamped writing pictures into clay.

Sometimes people cut letters into stone with a hammer and chisel.

Another way was to scratch lines into wax.

The Chinese used to paint letters with a brush and ink.

SAND FOR DRYING INK

Then people learnt to write with pens made from bird's feathers. These were called quill pens.

Goose feather pen

Crow feather pen

Goose feathers were best for writing. Swan and turkey feathers were good too. If you wanted to make thin lines, you had to use a crow feather pen.

Pencils

The first pencils were just chunks of graphite.

Then people wrapped the graphite in string.

Then they covered it with wood.

INK IS STORED IN HERE

THIN PIPE FOR INK

INK ON NIB

abcde

Then people used pens with steel nibs. Later fountain pens were invented. They are better than dip pens because they have a store of ink.

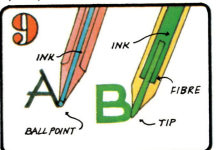

INK   INK

A   B

BALL POINT   TIP   FIBRE

Now there are pens that you do not have to fill up at all, like ball point pens and felt-tipped pens.

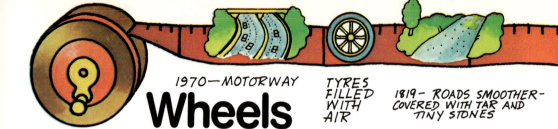

Wheels

TYRES
FILLED
WITH
AIR

1819— ROADS SMOOTHER—
COVERED WITH TAR AND
TINY STONES

COACH WITH
LEATHER STRAPS
FOR SPRINGS

Wheels for Carrying and Travelling

3500 B.C.
1ST
POTTER'S
WHEEL

In the beginning, there were no carriages or carts. Travellers walked or rode on an animal, carrying their luggage themselves. Sometimes travellers pulled their luggage along on a branch. Sometimes they put it on a sort of sledge.

3500 B.C.
1ST WHEEL

2000 B.C.
WHEEL
WITH
SPOKES

Sometimes it was easier to push really heavy things along on rollers, like this.

Then people learnt to make wheels. The wheels were very heavy, because they were made of solid wood. They could not have turned very fast.

Wheels became much lighter when people made them with spokes and rims.

POTTER'S
WHEEL
WITH
PEDAL

Travelling was quicker on good roads. The Romans built miles and miles of roads. The roads often had paving stones on them.

Travelling became smoother when people thought of making springs. The first springs were leather straps.

Then came the rubber tyre filled with air. Roads became smoother too, when people started to cover them with tar and many tiny stones.

3000 YEARS AGO

85 B.C.—
1ST WATER WHEEL

POST
WINDMILL

VERY BAD,
BUMPY
ROADS IN
EUROPE

1000 YEARS AGO

Wheels for Making Pots

Before the potters' wheel was invented, it was difficult to make round pots. People made pots by shaping lumps of clay.

Then somebody put a wheel on its side and put clay on it. All the potter had to do was turn the wheel. He could make round pots more easily.

It became even easier when the potter did not have to turn the wheel with his hands. He just pressed a pedal with his foot and the wheel turned.

Wheels for Grinding

WHEEL TURNS
THIS WAY

WATER GOES
THIS WAY

THE WINDMILL
CAN TURN TO
FACE THE
WIND

Grinding grain was a very long, tiring job. People or animals had to spend long hours turning the top mill stone round to grind the grain underneath.

Then somebody tried to make water do the work instead. He made a water wheel turn and this moved the grind stone round.

Then somebody tried using wind instead of water. The wind made the sails of a windmill turn like a giant wheel and the mill stones turned around inside.

2000 YEARS AGO

ROMAN ROADS

Word Index

The numbers show you the pages where you can read about each invention.

Picture Index

The numbers show you the pages where you can find the things in the pictures.

Invent your Way to the Moon

This is a game where your inventors race to invent their way right through history to land on the Moon. If you are unlucky, they can get stuck for a long time at one level of invention.

For counters, use small coins, buttons or little circles of cardboard.

THE MOON

WIRELESS

TELEVISION

SATELLITE

ROCKET

CAMERA

TRAIN

TELEGRAPH

STEAM CARRIAGE

BICYCLE

POWERED SHIP

GUNS

CANDLES

BOWS AND ARROWS

ALPHABET

START

THE WHEEL

SHADOW CLOCK

This is a race to the Moon for 2 players. Each player has 2 counters. Each counter stands for an inventor. The first player to get both his inventors to the Moon wins.

Throw the dice to see how many boxes you can move. Take it in turns to throw the dice. Each turn, you must move one of your inventors sideways along the row he is on in either direction. If an inventor reaches the end of his row, he must turn round and come back along the row until he has moved the full number on the dice. If an inventor ends his turn on a box with an arrow, he moves straight up to the box above.

If an inventor lands on the same box as any other inventor, the first one there, whichever side he is on, must move down a row to the box with a yellow frame. If the yellow-framed box has an inventor on it, that inventor too moves down a row to another box with a yellow frame.

Inventors can pass through boxes with other inventors on them. When an inventor lands on the Rocket Box, the player must throw a 6 to get lift-off to land on the Moon. An inventor already on the Rocket Box does not have to move unless another inventor lands on it. Then the first one moves down a row to a yellow-framed box.

PRINTED IN BELGIUM

proost Turnhout (Belgium)